Copyright © 2023 N

ALL RIGHTS RES
Notice of Copy
This book is a work of fiction. Names, characters, business organizations, places, events and incidents either are the product of the author's imagination or are used fictitiously. Any resemblance to actual persons, living or dead, events or locales is entirely coincidental.
Cover by: Ash Ericmore
Edited by 360 Editing (A division of Uncomfortably Dark)
Editor: Candace Nola

ISBN: 9798394675218

To Stuart

Thanks for Being Awesome ♡

To Stuart

Thanks for
Being Awesome

[signature]

CONTENTS

Copyright
1:	2
2:	7
3:	10
4:	17
5:	21
6:	24
7:	28
8:	31
9:	36
10:	41
11:	47
12:	51
13:	55
14:	58
15:	61
About The Author	68

Prologue:

Can you imagine living a life where pain is all you know? Where every part of your body aches and the pain is so bad some days you cannot get out of bed. Appointment after appointment, you have no answers, and end up waiting for someone to save you from the nightmare?

What if salvation was offered to you, a way out from the horrors of life, where you don't have to end it all?

Would you take it? No matter how high or how terrible the cost. Could you do the worst, to ease your own pain?

Let me tell you my story...

1:

"Just kill the guy already," the voice in my head whines incessantly.

"No, we need him."

"The guys a quack. He just said the only solution is to have a baby?!"

I hear the doctor's conversation over the barrage of abuse being hurled at me over and over again; I feel like my head is going to explode.

I clutch my head in my hands and I feel a warm hand on my shoulder, which startles me back to reality.

"I am sorry, Miss Roberts, but until Gynaecology gets back to me, stick to your regular medications," Dr Das insists.

He has been my doctor for over two years now, and nothing seems to change. I'm stuck between a rock and a hard place. The pain has even started affecting work. It was last week that I started to hear voices. It got worse when I stopped my meds. One voice, however, is always dominate.

Her Voice.

A feminine voice that holds authority in my mind, screaming at me until I finally listen to what she has to say. The catch is the voice only seems to be more vocal when I am in the most pain.

Today is no different. Even getting up this morning was hell on earth. I wanted to crawl back into bed and forget the world, but she won't let me.

I have no idea why I even make appointments for the same disappointing news. The same suggested treatment that does nothing to help.

"You had an operation last year, and the endo tissue was removed. I don't know what more you want us to do."

Dr Das has a slither of irritation in his voice as he types loudly on his computer keyboard.

"Yeah, well, what does he think woke me up?" She sneers. I am actually glad I am the only one that hears her.

I can feel my pelvic muscles tighten, and pain shoots up to my stomach like a lightning bolt, forcing me to double over in front of the doctor. I hear him release a loud sigh, which makes me want to punch him.

"Just keep taking the painkillers and it will calm down."

"Does this look like it is calming down?" I cry out.

For the first time in months, I explode.

First, he tells me to keep up with the pain meds, then he tells me not to because of the risk of addiction. NOW he tells me I can't have an operation to check if it has grown back for another year?!

How does he expect me to respond?

"We can send you for an ultrasound or MRI, but the waiting list is just as long."

"Oh, of course, the two types of tests that *won't* show endo!" I snap.

"Miss Roberts, there is only so much I can do and even then, we need confirmation from the Gynaecology department, which is currently a year and half behind because of Covid."

"He does know mansplaining the same thing from earlier won't help, right?" She mocks loudly in my skull.

"You know what? I am done. I will have to go private because I have no idea where my national insurance goes. Because it obviously isn't to help with treatment or getting a damn appointment!"

My voice echoes through the room, booming around my ears, and, no doubt, his. At which point, he rises from his chair and points a finger towards the door.

Before another word leaves his lips, I am already out of my chair and slamming the door behind me. Tears stream down my face as I race out of the doctor's office, feeling hopeless and abandoned.

Until she speaks again.

"It's not over yet, my friend."

***

The rain hits hard, turning the sky from blue to grey. It seems to be only getting darker to match my mood. I can't stop crying. The tears flow freely down my cheeks as I consider all the time this condition has taken from me. My muscles cling together and the pain surges through me like venom, making my stomach twist. I want to fall to my knees in the middle of the streets, begging to be spared, but I know what comes next.

I feel the sharp stabbing pain in my vagina, and then a warm sensation between my legs, but the pain has brought a friend. I am almost home. The burning sensation in my back is telling me it is coming. I make it into the lift.

Thank God no one is here, I think as I push the button over and over. Finally, the doors close shut and my bowels release.

Wailing in pain as the blood seeps into my trousers, the smell of metal mixed with crap hits my nose and surrounds me.

"Smell that? That's you. Embrace it," the voice teases.

My nose wrinkles as it hits all five senses, but then the doors of the lift open.

I pray that there is no one on the other side.

The hallway is empty, and I thank whatever deity allowed it. I waddle to my flat and unlock the front door.

The keys jingle in my hands, alerting the dog next door to my presence. The sound of my sobbing is drowned out by constant husky barks from across the hall.

Finally, I make it through the door, falling through and landing on the cold concrete floor. For the first time since living here, I am glad I had not laid the carpet yet.

I lie there trying to catch my breath as laughter echoes through my mind. I can feel the blood and shit pooling in my underwear, running down my legs, saturating my jeans. The pain has me paralysed to the floor. All I can do is lie there while my ovaries rage and my stomach turn inside out. I crawl to the bathroom, but the pain hits my legs and cripples me before travelling up my back.

Blood was pouring from my vagina and my ass as I screamed in agony, my arms flopping to the side. I pray for release, to be spared from the ongoing agony.

But my prayer is unanswered.

Now I beg for death on the cold floor of my hallway.

That is when *she* answers me.

"I can make the pain stop," she whispers.

I wonder if my mind is seriously cruel enough to offer me hope, by psychosis. Am I having a mental break finally? After years of torment? Or is this all really in my head? The pain and the blood are not there, maybe.

But the smell of faeces is real enough, as diarrhoea continues to leak onto the floor mixing with my blood, creating a putrid deadly stench.

"Let me help you, I can take all this away," she purrs in my mind.

The pain eases slightly as she makes her promise to me. I can finally speak without crying and I ask.

"How?"

She only gives me one sentence, one that I will never forget as long as I live. This will be the day that I finally left sanity behind and embraced the madness.

FREE ME.

2:

I finally had a name for the voice in my head, Meigs.

Or rather, that is the name she liked to call herself. Meigs convinced me that if I helped free her, she would leave my body and never come back. Either the blood loss had affected my brain, or I was actually speaking to something living inside my body.

I can still feel blood gushing between my legs. My jeans have gone from blue to a deep navy mixed with crimson.

Psychological or not, as soon as I agreed, the pain abruptly became a dull ache, and the bleeding screeched to a halt. Meaning I could finally get out of the mess on the floor. Stumbling like a newborn deer out of my filth, I head for the toilet door and clean myself up in the sink. I can't look at myself in the mirror. I don't want to see the filth and grime pouring into the sink as I peel away my jeans.

The smell is going to take hours to get rid of. If the neighbours come knocking, I would have to make some excuse.

Almost as if on cue, I hear scratching at the door frame, the usual telltale sign that I have my favourite guest at the threshold. But today I am not ready to be dived on by a large dog. I am not up for any contact, to be honest. I can hear her whining behind the wooden door. Honestly, it's breaking my heart. But I know if I let her in, the carer from across the hall might call an ambulance once she sees the amount of blood soaking into the floor. Once I hear the scratching stop, and the sound of dog paws smacking against the tiled hallway, I know she must have been called back in by her owner. No doubt disappointed.

After scrubbing my skin raw, using all manner of cleaning products, I finally felt human again. Meigs was quiet. This was unnerving.

But it gave me time to reclaim the dignity I just lost. Now, it was time for the hard part, cleaning my filth off the concrete floor. I grab the mop and bucket from the cupboard and get to work; a fresh burst of energy surging through my veins. By the time I finish with the mop, I grab the scrubbing brush to be extra sure. My hands are cut and bleeding, but I don't care. It's a welcome distraction from the nagging ache in my body.

The flat stinks of pure bleach and disinfectant. I swear this could pass for a hospital inspection now. I stand up, still shaking, unable to comprehend what the fuck was going on.

Am I dreaming? Is this a nightmare I have not woken up from yet?

"Don't you wish it was that simple," Meigs responds.

"What do you want from me?"

"I told you; I want to be free. But I will need your help."

I walk over to the window and pull a cigarette off the side with my lighter. I need a moment to think. To really consider what the hell is going on here, but no matter how much I inhale of the smoky tobacco, nothing brings me relief.

A sudden surge of pain rushes up through my leg to my ovaries. I drop my cigarette to the side and grasp my waist.

"Now I have your full, undivided attention. I believe we should talk next steps," Meigs' voice growls in my head.

"*Shit,*" I drop down and pick the cigarette up off the floor, managing not to burn a hole in the lino. I stub it out quickly.

"Tonight, we will go out."

The demand is seared into my mind like a map. I feel the urge to leave the flat against my better judgment. Especially in this area, it is dangerous to go out at night, wandering around in the dark could lead to being mugged or worse.

"Just trust me, after tonight you will wish you agreed to me sooner."

I ... need to rest, to breathe, to dream away from this.

"Then go to sleep, Cali, because tonight, you will need your strength. And a sharp knife."

3:

I wake up to the sensation of bile burning my throat.
Fuck, I forgot to take my antacid medication.
I jump out of bed as I feel the sensation getting worse. I run out and reach the toilet bowl in time. Vomit surges from my mouth and clings to the basin. Chunks of this morning's breakfast fill the waters. Floating around on the surface, the smell hits me first and I try to hold back another surge of vomit. Tears fill my eyes; I beg for this to stop, but another flood of vomit fills the toilet, but this time, the bile has a green tint to it.

I pull back, horrified at the sight before me. I shuffle backwards on my knees.

"Oh, don't mind that," her voice springs into my head. "You will get used to it soon enough."

"What the fuck was that?"

"Just some internal plumbing being reworked," she sniggers.

"I have never vomited anything like this shit before! Christ, it smells like off pickled onion!"

"Preparation… now get your coat. It's cold out tonight."

"What the hell for?"

I realise in that moment when a lightening shock surges through my body, that was the wrong question to ask.

I fall onto my back, nearly cracking my fucking head off the floor because of the force. When I lift myself up, I swear I can see stars across my eyes. *Fuck's sake, did I give myself a concussion?*

"Not yet, but if you keep answering me back, you won't get back up again," the voice hisses in my rattled brain.

"Fine, fine. But. Where are we going?"

After a moment of silence, she hums in my head.

"A walk," she simply says to me.

I feel nausea flush through me again and end up throwing my face back into the toilet bowl.

***

After what feels like forever, hurling my guts up in the bathroom. I stumble towards the cupboard and pull out my coat. I've put on a bit of weight since I brought it, with the amount of medicine I am on there is no surprise, really. I went from a healthy eight stone and shot up to thirteen stone in a matter of months. No diet plan or fasting could change things.

No matter what I ate or how much sleep I got, the weight stayed on, which resulted in me struggling to fasten the zipper on my black coat. I could feel Meigs' disgust in me. The emotion infects my being to the point that I give up, leaving it half zipped and move on to my shoes.

I hear a silent hiss coming from between my legs, then I feel it. Something slithering around the inside of my thigh. I pull up the bottom of the coat to check. Nothing unusual. My legs look the same and nothing inside my leggings.

But I can still feel it, a prickling sensation now as it moves around my hip and circles around my lower back. Like something is trying to wrap its body around my waist, the sudden sharp scratching takes my breath away.

It takes a moment, but I finally regain focus. I can hear them. The voices in my head, whispering in my mind, but not loud enough for me to make out what they are saying. The lights flicker, turning my kitchen into a makeshift rave as I feel the ground shift beneath my boots. It feels like something is alive, moving beneath my soles. I look down and the ground looks like it's moving, various colours circling the floor. I feel like I'm watching a group of snakes wrestling across the lino.

Locked in a trance with the rainbow of colours, I feel calm and at ease. Until I hear her voice ring out in my mind, clear as a bell.

"It is time. Let's go Cali."

I do not question her or answer her back. I simply walk across the room to the door, head down the hallway, and reach for my keys in the lock. My body seems to be set on autopilot, like I'm following instructions already placed out in my mind. I turn the key and exit the flat. The rest of my journey is a blur. I can't remember getting in the lift or getting out at the bottom. In the time it takes me to blink, I am standing in complete darkness halfway up an alleyway that I usually take to get to town. The air is brisk; the wind snapping at my cheeks as the rain hammers down violently across the pavement. It seems the downpour has continued all the way into the night; I check my pockets.

No phone and no wallet. Just my keys.

Fuck. If I need help, I am so screwed!

"You will be fine," her voice is smooth as silk.

I cannot help but obey the unspoken command and carry on walking, deeper into the darkness, out of the safety of the streetlights. I carry on into the rainstorm, my coat slowly filling up with water as the ice-cold wind snaps at my throat. You know, one of those nights where it is so damn cold that it hurts your throat to breathe? That is what tonight feels like. I wanted to go back the moment I stepped outside, but she was adamant and persistent.

It is obey and keep walking into the pitch black or go back and suffer a night of unbearable torture at her…

Hands? No, I have no fucking idea what she has? But either way, she would make me pay for defying her. I do not doubt that.

I know she can hear my thoughts; she knows I won't run back and has full control over me, so I may as well play along and see where this takes me.

In fact, I do not recognise this area at all now? How long have I been walking, actually? A mile, no, it can't be that long, but…

I look over my shoulder and turn fully around to see where I have actually come from. I see a dark muddy path, trees all around me in a state of nakedness from the time of the year. I am in the middle of the park, not just any park, either.

This park has a reputation, which is why no one in their right mind would even dream of travelling here during the day, let alone the dead of the night.

My attention snaps back as I hear movement coming from behind me, the crunching sound of leaves underfoot and I start power walking my way out the woods.

The ligaments in my legs tighten when I feel a presence getting closer and I hear their muddy footsteps increase, so I speed up my pace.

A part of me wants to run back home to the safety of my flat. My heart is pounding in my ears like a drum as they chase me through the darkness. I can see a streetlamp up ahead. I am almost there, almost on the pavement, which means I will be in the light's safety once more and out of this moment.

I feel a hand snatch my wrist, and all my hope vanishes in a second. I face my stalker and see they have a bandana covering half their face with their hoody up to conceal the rest of their features. I stand there, as if watching stock motion as they pull back their other hand. It was not a light love tap either. They full on belted me hard across the cheek. Sparks of lights hit my eyes; I feel the skin under my eye swell up immediately.

"Gimme your phone," they growl in a low tone. They then take both hands and grab me by my jacket collar. I don't know whether to be shocked or impressed they have the strength to lift me. My back smacks against the bark of the tree and they pull me forward again, just to smash my spine back into the tree.

"BLUD? YOU DEAF? YA PHONE AND YOUR WALLET!"

The rain has calmed down, and I can hear more clearly without the rain thumping against my hood.

Their voice sounds a little less gruff now, like they were putting on a voice all along. I finally have the courage now to answer back and make eye contact with my attacker.

"I... didn't bring it. I don't have anything."

Yeah, I knew the moment those words left my lips I was going to regret saying them.

The rage in their eyes said everything. As they step to the side, a slither of light hits them. The more I looked into their eyes, the more details I could make out. I could see the smeared bits of black eyeliner and false lashes clearer now; I think she notices this and steps back into the shadows. Slipping a hand into her pocket, she pulls out a small Stanley knife.

Fuck... I am so dead.

I watch as she runs at me and brace for the pain of the blade. Two seconds pass, nothing. I open my eyes and cannot believe what the fuck is happening.

The knife is gone from her hands, vanished out of sight. I have my hands around her throat, and I am choking the life out of her.

Bear in mind, I have no control over my body at this point. It is like I can see what is happening. I can feel the pressure increase as I squeeze her throat in my grasp. But I can't fucking stop myself. I have no idea what is going on. I am a visitor in my own body, just watching on in horror.

I see the blood trickle out of her eyes, as she gasps for breath frantically while clawing at my hands with her manicured nails.

I cannot help but think *wait if you can afford to get your nails done, which must be around fifty pounds, easy? Why the fuck are you out late at night robbing me, a person who has never had their nails done?*

The whimpering sound from her lips along with the sensation of warm fluid pouring over my hands brings me back to the carnage at hand.

Wow, that was a badly timed pun.

Even dark humour could not cover up the genuine terror I am feeling in this moment as blood spurts from her nose, her ears, and her eyes. I had no idea this leave of strength even existed in my body, let alone the strength to strangle someone to death.

Why cannot I stop myself?? What the hell is happening? I am going to kill her.

"Oh, for fuck's sake, stop being such a baby. In fact, let's end this game of cat-and-mouse bullshit."

That voice, it is coming from my mouth; it is my voice, and my lips were moving. But I never spoke. I have no way of saying anything... it must have been. No.

No, no, no, no, she... can't. How could she?

"Yep, it's me, because you could not even do a tiny bit of self-defence. I had to step in."

She is gloating, the bitch is genuinely gloating while she almost snaps the life out of this girl.

My focus is back, my thoughts quiet, and I watch Meigs operating my body while I am trapped inside my mind, a spectator.

My hand reaches forward and grabs the cartilage in the centre of the girl's neck. I can feel my nails to dig into the skin and clawing into the muscles surrounding her windpipe. She tries to scream out, but in one quick and brutally swift movement, I have removed her trachea from her neck.

The bloody cartilage wiggles side to side in my palm, blood gushes from the open wound, and my body casually steps aside. The girl lands face first on the ground, barely making a sound in the empty woods as the gargling sound continues for a few more minutes before stopping altogether.

"That was fun. It's been a while since I've been able to do that," Meigs boasts.

My head feels weird. My vision blurs, and I realise I am back in possession of my body once more, but right now I really wish I wasn't.

I throw aside the sticky, blood-soaked thing that was in my hand and start wiping my hands across my coat. The blood is still warm on my hands. I can still see bits of muscle and flesh under my fingernails.

I can't help it; I drop to my knees next to the grotesque scene and just sob. Meigs is back in the back my mind, berating me, and huffing at my 'emotional display.'

"Oh god, oh god, what have I done? What did I do?" I whimper on my hands and knees. I reach out cautiously and roll the body onto her back.

Her bandana has come completely off her face, and her hood has fallen down. Her eyes are like saucers staring into death and her mouth is still wide from the scream that she did not have time to make.

"You. You're a monster," I spit.

"Oh, sweet child, and now… so are you."

4:

I kneel in the wet mud; my hands are covered with her blood. I don't know what to do next, this is a fucking nightmare. I want to throw up. The smell of iron mixes with something stronger.

Oh God, did her bowels release? Now I can feel the bile rising in my throat.

"Don't you **dare**," I hear her threaten. "You want to give them DNA?"

"They have my fingerprints all over her. She has practically taken a bath in my fucking DNA?!"

"That won't be an issue, but if you throw up next to her, then they *will* have DNA."

I don't ask what she means by that statement, but I won't press the matter. All I want now is to wash away the evidence of tonight's horrors.

Then, as if answering my prayers, I hear the thunder rumble above my head and the downpour starts again. I look up to the sky, embracing the rain as it pours across my blood-soaked face. The cold air stings my cheek.

That bitch really gave me a shiner. Covering this up is going to be fun.

I reach my hands up to the sky and let the crimson colour pour over my palms, dripping down into the mud. Blood with blood. As her body lies in a bed of brown and black leaves, I notice her arm twisted around a branch. Then I realise it's not a branch. It's her bone sticking out of her arm from where she fell onto a stone slab, barely visible in the dim light. The only reason I can see it now is because the water is washing the dirt aside to reveal the hard, cold surface of the world.

I want to get up and walk away from the scene laid out in front of me, but like a car wreck, I cannot look away.

And she knows it.

I snap out of the trance long enough to pull myself off the ground. The sludgy mess sticks to my jeans as I realise the blood has imprinted onto the material where I pressed my hands onto my thighs.

At this moment, I look like Bambi, with barely the strength in my legs to hold myself up, and my hands are still shaking. My anxiety is off the charts. I can feel my heart beating against my throat, you know, the thing this girl doesn't have anymore. The pangs of guilt are snapping at me. My hair is soaked, I am freezing cold. I should really leave. This very second, I need to go home. I want to leave.

"Not yet," she whispers.

"What?"

"We still have so much left to do," Meigs purrs, sending a shiver down my spine.

"Jesus Christ, Meigs, what more do you want?"

Oh, great, now I am speaking aloud to the damn thing.

"I know you're hungry, so am I."

There it is again, that mind-numbing panic setting in. I know, God, I know in my core what she wants, but I still need to ask that dumb ass question to be sure.

"Well, yeah, I am, but I can grab something at home."

The laughter in my head is deafening.

"And waste a perfectly satisfying meal? I mean, she is not gonna need them anymore?"

"What the hell do you expect me to do here!? No, I won't do it whatever the fuck you want. I won't do it!"

"Even if it will help keep the pain at bay?"

Fuck, I did not expect that.

"What do you mean?"

I swear to God if this thing has a face under that bone and muscle down there, I guarantee it is smiling up at me right now.

"Well, she's already turned over, and the 'obstruction' has been removed."

Meigs sounds gleeful, proud of the carcass that will soon be rotting into the ground the next day. I feel like a snake has tightened its coils around my spine and I hear in my mind the sound of a pained hiss.

"Look closer at the throat. You know anatomy, you've read enough horror. What do you think I am looking for?"

The truth is, I don't know what I'm looking for; the darkness is making it hard to see anything. The only bit of light that does come through is from the streetlight, but even with the rain thrashing my face, I have no clue what she could be talking about.

"It's gore, blood, and slashed fleshed. What the hell is so important that I need to subject my stomach to it?"

"Bad move, Cali."

Before I have a chance to question what she means, pain bursts downward through my lower abdomen. It is like a crowbar has been smashed right through to my tibia on both legs. Bringing me to my knees by the girl's body again. My kneecaps ache. I am at the age now where I get sore just kneeling. This will leave a massive bruise.

"How about I guide you?" Meigs growls.

I can tell she is pissed now. The irritation in her voice is hard to ignore and I can feel the waves of pain radiating as I move my hands towards the torso of the body. I go higher and the pain lessens; I move down and it intensifies again. It feels like a game of hot and cold. The closer I get to what she wants, the less the pain is.

I get to the part where the massive cavern is, a large hole where the trachea used to be, and my fingertips vibrate. As if homing in on something beneath the flat of skin right under the chin, I feel the pain calm down completely as I lift it aside.

I see that the top piece of the windpipe is still there. I mean, the voice box is gone but there is a butterfly shaped piece of squishy tissue. It must have been behind her windpipe, only when it was removed was it not visible.

"That is the thyroid gland, that produces hormones and that is what I need. So, eat up. We do not have much time left."

Uhhhh God no

"Sorry Cali, no back seating now. Either you're in or I can make you live through pain that will make you wish I killed you."

The threat is enough. Megi's isn't playing around. It didn't look all that appetising. I gingerly reach in and pluck the glands from what is left of the cartilage. It wiggles between my fingers, and I can already tell this is going to have the texture of rubber just by how it feels.

So here I am, making a choice. Not a great choice, but hey, how many more mistakes and fuck-ups can I pile into tonight?

Callie Roberts, the girl who got constantly beat up in high school, is now about to eat the remains of a girl she murdered with her bare hands. You cannot make this shit up, I mean, how the hell did I go from workaholic chronic illness bitch to cold-blooded murderer over night?

Oh, Christ, that is what the newspapers will say! Spread across the front pages of social media for all to see, London's new killer!

"Just shut the fuck up and eat the gland so we can get back, I am fucking freezing!"

Her demand is hard to ignore. I split it into two pieces to make the chunks smaller to swallow.

"One… two… three,"

Down the hatch it goes and, oh god, I want to be sick immediately. It has the feel of uncooked liver as it slides down the back of my throat. I want to throw it back up, but stop myself, coughing twice to cover the discomfort of what just slithered into my body.

"Get used to it. I am nowhere near done with you."

5:

I wish I could say I didn't enjoy scoffing down that grisly chunk. But I swiftly moved on to the next piece, when I realised the effect it was having on me.

It's weird, but I'm having a moment of pure bliss. No pain, no aches. I mean, it doesn't even taste that bad. I feel like I'm floating as I walk. My feet seem to carry me in the right direction at least, and my walking speed has increased.

I'm not out of breath or stopping to wince every five seconds. I feel normal; I feel human again even though what I just did was far from human. Only ten minutes ago, I was digging through the remains of a girl who tried to rob me, that I killed with my bare hands and no weapons.

It starts me thinking about the voice inside my body. What is her goal? I say her but who knows... it's better than calling Meigs 'it' or 'the thing inside my vagina'. *Actually, I'm pretty sure I read a story about a woman with an entire world inside her vagina. So, I guess this isn't that strange?*

I've been walking for ages now, and my legs aren't even tired. The speed I'm moving at, I will be home before daybreak. I still can't believe I spent an entire night out in the middle of the most dangerous area in the neighbourhood and survived. But I know I can't take all the credit; I need to speak to her. I can't just bury my head in the sand until the next time she gets a murderous impulse.

My legs carry my body on autopilot, as if on a mission. I know what mission that is, to lie the fuck down. I could feel my body getting heavy, my stomach gurgling as I approach the tower block. My cell but also my sanctuary. It has to be early morning now. I can hear the birds singing in the sky, which means I need to get inside.

I step into the foyer, my hands shaking as I run towards the lift.

Oh great, that will irritate my stomach more.

The lift doors open and I dive in, pounding the floor number to force the doors closed. The pain makes its way up my legs to my abdomen, and I hold back the cry of pain.

Every fucking morning is like clockwork.

The longest lift ride in eternity ensues as it makes its way to my floor. I look back at the mirror behind me. Dirt streaks my face as if I went on a muddy obstacle course. I need to wash, but first, I must release the demons thrashing around in my bowels. I feel the pain again. My urgency forces me out of the lift and to my front door. One step is all it took. The hallway resonates with the sound of my neighbour's dog barking. Scrambling for my keys, I can hear the incessant howling. The sound cloaks the roaring from within; I fly through the door and lock it behind me.

My salvation is on my right. I can still hear the barking as I yank my pants down and drop onto the toilet. My bowels open and my guts feel like they're falling into the toilet. Intense and painful bowel movements, the doctors call it.

I call it intense fire from my ass, as the toilet bowl fills with blood and shit. I get no release though. The sound echoes around me and the smell is horrific. But what did I think would happen? I just ate part of a person; it wasn't going to cure me.

"No, not yet," Meigs whispers, her voice being given more volume by the acoustics of the bathroom.

I ignore the comment and let my body expel the waste, hoping it will clear some part of my soul after what just took place. When it finally stops, I look down to wipe and tremble at the sight beneath me. The once-white bowl is now filled with solid black with putrid liquid slashed up the sides. I look at the sludge, disgusted. I know this is not normal. I should call a doctor or, more appropriately, an ambulance. But instead, I wipe and flush, then wash my hands and pretend it never happened. I fall face down on the bed, still in my muddy clothes and boots, and let the darkness take hold.

6:

My eyes open to no source of light, and I turn away from the bed to the side table. I reach out blindly for my phone, which I left on the standby the light last night.

I click the side, and the screen illuminates the room, burning my eyes. I'm shocked to see the time and date.

It is midnight, and it is Wednesday. I've slept through an entire day. The second thing I notice is the smell of my clothes, an earthy smell mixed with a strong body odour. I've been asleep in these for a whole day. My skin crawls just thinking about it, then another realisation hits me as I swing my legs round and turn on the light.

For the first time, I do not see a blood patch. Usually by now, I would have a massive bloody impression stained across my groin, but this time, nothing. I get up and run to the bathroom, to be certain.

Sure enough, I pull down my pants and not even a drop of blood is on my liner.

I can't even remember the last time I looked down into my underwear and didn't see blood starting back at me.

I decided to test another theory and go to the toilet for a wee. No pain. Usually, I cannot hold my bladder for more than three hours without needing a very painful piss. But all I feel is relief after emptying my bladder.

"I told you."

"You're still here?"

"Of course, you idiot. I am part of you, after all. Where am I going to go?" she sneers.

So, there is no escape then. Unless I decide to somehow convince my consultant to take me seriously. But let's be serious, even if I did, they would more than likely lock me up for hearing voices. It took them 10 years to diagnose this damn endometriosis. I thought getting diagnosed would help. Instead, they just gave me a load of drugs and sent me on my way. No follow-up, and no checks to see if the surgery was a success. Nothing.

"That reminds me, when did you last take your pain medication?"

"Sometime Tuesday," the answer I gave surprised me.

It's the first time in years that I have had a pain-free day. I cannot remember a day when I wasn't popping pain meds.

"A whole day, huh? Guess that should be proof enough that I want to help you," Meigs scoffs.

So, eating that thing from the girl? That helped? No, that can't be the case. I can't justify murdering someone, not for a day of relief.

If I went to the Doctor and told them anything, it would just convince them, it is all in my head. They already have me off work sick because they have nothing else to recommend for the pain. They told me if it was affecting my life so badly, I shouldn't work until they had time to investigate it. Which was code for 'waiting for a hospital appointment', which could mean months. So, if this thing will help me, that's more than the so-called professionals have done for me.

"I bet that is the best night's sleep you have had in months," she purrs.

The truth is yes, because I could not remember my dreams. I actually felt well-rested.

"Now you have proof that I keep my word. All I want to do is help. I want to take the pain away."

"Yeah, but at what cost? Murder? I will not kill someone to relieve my pain."

I knew at that moment my insubordination would cost me. Right on cue, an electric shock hit my pelvis, and I collapsed on the side of the bath. A sharp crunch on impact leaves me struggling to breathe. I pull myself up, careful not to do anymore damage, and lift my shirt to check.

The swelling has already started, and the skin is turning a dark blue. Spider webs of purple are forming under my ribs, from where I hit the side. I trace my fingertips over the lines and wince at the pain.

"Pathetic, you honestly think you have any chance of standing against me?" she spat.

"I won't do it; I won't kill anyone."

"What have you seriously got to lose? Right now, you can barely make it through one day without collapsing into tears. All you know is pain."

"There are people facing worse than me, hell there are people going through cancer. Terminal, I'm lucky to be alive."

"You call this 'living' spending your days huddled up in bed?" She scoffs. "You spend every day in pain or on the toilet."

She's not wrong. Whenever the pain gets so bad, I can barely move. It takes all my energy just to leave my bed to go to the toilet. This is not living; I've gained so much weight due to all the tablets. You can forget about exercise, just taking the stairs kills me. I have zero stamina, or concentration, and only want to sleep. But of course, she knows that.

She is in my fucking head.

"Accept it. You need me, Cali."

I need to distract myself. So, I strip as she berates me in my mind. As I tug off my trousers and underwear, I look down and feel all my willpower leave me. Tears form in the corner of my eyes, just looking at the scars across my thighs.

She is right. What have I got to lose? No. I won't give in to the insanity, I am stronger than this.

"For now."

7:

After scrubbing my body raw, I clean the dredges of brown and red around the plughole. Even having a shower is exhausting. My whole body feels like I just ran a marathon.

As I wrap the towel around my body, I notice the bruising is coming out more under my ribs. Taking on a purple hue, it has swollen to where it looks like a small balloon under my rib cage. I head to the kitchen to boil the kettle; the pelvic pain is starting up again. While it doesn't stop the pain, a boiling hot water bottle on my thighs is a welcome distraction. The kettle thunders to life as the steam pours from the top. I grab my water bottle and fill it halfway. Then drag my body to the sofa, where I collapse and let the soft fabric envelop me.

"You know that won't do shit," she sneers.

"Shut up, I don't want to hear it," I snap, as I direct my anger between my legs.

I thrust the water bottle violently onto my vagina, the heat burns my skin. I haven't even bothered putting on underwear, hoping the searing hot rubber will reduce the nettles shifting inside my ovaries. It helps for about five minutes before the intense electrical current of pain vibrates through my pelvis. I stifle the scream rising from my throat, tears forming in my eyes as blinding pain hits my stomach. I won't give her the satisfaction of hearing my cries of agony, but she is already chuckling.

"I tried to warn you."

I hear a loud ding noise from across the room. My mind is still reeling but on the second vibration, I realise it's my phone. I push the bottle to the side and hobble to the kitchen counter where I left it.

No one calls or messages anymore, so who the hell would be contacting me this early?

I click the screen to see a text and an email that has to be spam. It wasn't.

To my utter shock, it was a hospital appointment for the next week. After months of waiting, they finally had me down for a consultation the next week. My eyes grew wide like saucers as I scanned the text, bewildered by the news. But also, for the first time in years, I had hope, though I was still in disbelief that this was real.

"You are so naïve," Meigs sneers. "You really think in one appointment they will solve anything? I didn't even show up on the last scan. What makes you think this will be any different?"

"It has to be," I whisper.

Her laughter is deafening. I feel like my eardrums are going to explode. My brain is on fire as she laughs hysterically. I fall to my knees and the towel falls away, exposing my naked body to the cold room. My operation scars on show for the entire world, along with the heat burns and knife marks on my legs.

"You have guts, I can't wait to pull them out," she threatens. "You are not my first woman, but I will be damn sure you are my last."

Her words are full of certainty. I can tell she means it.

"Fine. Keep living in ignorant bliss. Take your pills and herbal bullshit remedies. But I won't go away. You will see things my way soon enough."

For five days leading up to the appointment, she kept her promise. She made me suffer in ways I never thought possible. My stomach burned with fire, and the pain in my pelvis left me bed bound. I hardly ate anything and barely slept. When I slept, I was plagued with horrible nightmares. Visions of death beyond imagination, scenes of torture you would only ever see on the dark web. The waking world was no better. I cried so much that the skin under my eyes was so sore it hurt to keep them open. I begged and pleaded, but that only made her exact more pain from within me.

She was relentless, whether it was keeping me a slave to the toilet or crying in bed with a severe migraine. Meigs knew how to push the right buttons to keep breaking me down. It got too much by day three. I took a handful of Tramadol and forced them down my throat. Swallowing is hard, but I still emptied the packet down my throat. I just wanted out. I felt like there was no other option.

She had other plans.

Bitch made me throw them all straight back up again. I still remember the feel of the bile burning the back of my throat. The smell from the toilet basin as my eyes watered. Meigs made sure I would live. I couldn't die, not now, not while she still had control over me.

After I had emptied the contents of my stomach, I sobbed in the foetal position on the floor. Her laughter echoed in my mind as I wept like a child on the floor. I knew at that moment she had me right where she wanted me. Once my tears ran dry, I crawled back into bed and stayed there for the remainder of what felt like my prison sentence, with her as my cellmate.

My only hope now was that appointment. I said a little prayer in my head the night before.

8:

Finally, it's here. I sit in the taxi, an anxious mess as we pull up to the entrance. I get out and hear every bone in my body click. My throat is sore still and I won't even go into detail about why my back hurts. Everything that I had eaten the night before left my body violently this morning. Every step I take into the foyer is like walking on hot coals, especially since I now had two lumps growing on my labia. My thighs rubbing against the angry bumps makes the pain worse. I have to stand after checking in at reception; the anticipation is killing me and my legs ache. But sitting hurts more than words. It takes all my strength not to break down there and then.

I feel like I've been waiting an eternity, but it's only been 10 minutes.

God, please tell me this will be over.

"Moron," Meigs whispers, "so deluded, honestly, it's sad."

She is baiting me, trying to get a rise out of me. I look around and see others waiting in the seats set around the waiting room. I knew I had to ignore her. I doubt it will look good for me if I start arguing out loud with someone who isn't even there.

"Ohh, I see. Well, have it your way, Cali," Meigs spits.

"Calico Roberts."

I turn towards the doors to the back and see the nurse standing with a clipboard in her hands. She looks around inpatient, before letting out a sigh.

"Calico Roberts!"

Shit, that's me.

"Sorry, yes. Coming," I stammered, before rushing over to the nurse.

She opens the door and leads me through to the examination room on the left. The doctor is sitting reading some paperwork. Her eyes meet mine and she gives me a weak smile.

"Please Miss Roberts, I am Doctor Hedini. Please take a seat. I won't be a moment".

Her hand gestures to the seat nearest her desk, and I settle down opposite her. She continues glancing through the notes, her fingers tracing each word on the document. Dr Hedini stares intensely at the screen before addressing me.

The silence between us is unbearable.

When she speaks to me, the look in her eyes says everything. There is a pity in her expression as the Doctor looks me dead in the eyes. My hands shake and my leg bobs up and down.

"I have read the notes from your scan, Miss Roberts, and it shows nothing abnormal. This means that the Head consultant is reluctant to operate. I am sorry, but with your age and no evidence on the scan, he suggests another laparoscopy, but he is not willing to approve the hysterectomy, Miss Roberts. I would like to examine you to see if there are any changes. Would that be, ok?"

Fuck. Just fuck. I was so sure. So certain they would find something. They would at least see her.

"Miss Roberts?"

"Sorry, erm, yes, I'm happy to be examined. It's kind of got worse."

Her eyes now rest on my hands, clasping my stomach. That look crosses her face again, a mix of sadness and pity.

I hate that look. I don't want your pity; I want your help!

"Ok, if you can step behind the curtain and get undressed, I will be right there. I am just going to get a nurse," she announces, before leaving me alone in the room.

I wait until the door closes behind me before getting up. I just stand there, unable to move as I take in everything I have just been told. I want to break down, but there is still the examination. There might still be something that the doctor will find.

Please find something.

I finally snap out of my trance and step behind the curtain. I pull off my trousers and underwear, tossing them on the chair next to the bed. It hurts to sit; I swing my legs around so that I am lying down. I rest my head on the cushion and throw the tissue over my lap. Now I just have to lie there half-naked until she comes back into the room.

"I tried to tell you, I'm not some amateur you're dealing with."

I stare at the ceiling; any distraction is a welcome one from her incessant barrage of mental attacks. The one mark of the tile looks to be shaped like a heart; this doesn't bring me any comfort.

I hear the door open, and the curtain is pulled aside by Doctor Hedini, a meek young nurse standing beside her. The girl smiles at me, pushing her long dark hair behind her ear. The doctor walks silently over to the set of drawers and pulls out a speculum, the favoured torture device.

It looks like the mouth of a duck, but that's what goes into the opening of the vagina. The screws on the side are to make the opening wider so they can see inside. I hate it. I do everything I can to control my breathing, and the nurse covers the beak-shaped device in lube and directs a mini spotlight at my privates.

"Ok, Miss Roberts, take a deep breath for me, please."

I count to three with my eyes locked on the heart stain on the ceiling tile. The pain hits hard and I can feel the hard plastic inside me. I want to scream out into the room, as I feel the speculum pushing my opening wide open. Just a little longer. I just have to hang in a few minutes longer. Most people would pray for everything to be fine, but not me.

Please. Please see something. Anything can't be in my head. It has to be there. God, please see her.

I glance over to the end of the bed; the doctor seems to be focused on something. I look at the young nurse. Her name tag says 'Diana'. My eyes move to her face. Her expression has changed. Her face is white as a sheet, eyes wide with horror.

She looks terrified. Her hands cover her mouth and I look at the doctor. Her reaction is completely different. Neutral and unphased, but Diana is looking between my legs with fear plastered across her features. I watch as the poor girl's eyes roll into the back of her head, and she collapses. The sound of metal crashes to the floor and the doctor drops to the ground.

"OH MY GOD, DIANA, ARE YOU OK!?" Doctor Hedini cries out.

I try to sit up but realise the speculum is still inside me; my vagina retracts, and I hear a loud crunching noise between my legs. Something is stabbing me from the inside, like sharp pieces of broken glass.

"Oh God," the doctor whispers.

I didn't even notice her come back between my legs; she must have shot up from the ground when she heard the noise.

"Miss Roberts, please stay down. I need you to stay calm for me, but it looks like the speculum is trapped in your cervix."

I can tell her tone is an attempt at calm, but her words are shaky and panicked. My heart is in my throat as I feel her hand reach inside me. This is the first penetration of any form I've had in three years. I feel like my insides are being pulled apart. It's too much. I burst into tears as she rummages around inside me, pulling out piece after piece of the device lodged inside me.

"PLEASE, IT HURTS! STOP!' I beg.

"I promise, Miss Roberts, I am almost done. Please hold on," Doctor Hedini urges. "CAN I GET SOME HELP IN HERE!"

I hear the door fly open and an elderly nurse comes rushing in.

"Diana has passed out. Can you help her up? I need to get the speculum out of the patient. I can't do this while bending over her, please," Doctor Hedini commands.

I almost feel sorry for Diana, but right now I am more concerned about my well-being. I can feel myself getting overheated; my eyes grow heavy as I feel faint.

"I am nearly done, Miss Roberts. Please stay with me," she begs.

I try to stay focused, but like before, the black abyss invites me in, and I pass out.

9:

When I wake up, I see that I'm still lying down, but this time I am on a gurney. Wrapped in a warm blue blanket, I turn my head weakly to see where I am. I have been moved into a ward, and a blue curtain surrounds me. My head feels heavy every time I try to turn and my neck aches. I look down at my hand to find a button with a picture of a nurse on it, and on my wrist is an admission bracelet. It takes a moment, but I remember my ordeal and start smashing the button with my thumb. The elderly nurse from before comes around the curtain and smiles at me.

"You gave us quite a scare, Miss Roberts. How are you feeling?"

"Sore," I croak, "What happened?"

She seems reluctant to answer my question as she bites her bottom lip.

"Let me get Doctor Hedini. She will explain."

Before I can ask any more questions, she disappears.

What the fuck happened? Why did that nurse faint? What did she see inside of me when they did the exam? How the hell did the speculum get stuck?

I hear the curtain rustle open and the Doctor steps out from behind it. Her eyes are full of genuine concern as she reaches my bedside.

"Miss Robert, I am so sorry for what happened downstairs. It seems the nurse I asked to chaperone was not feeling too well and passed out. I am so sorry. I had no idea. When you panicked, your pelvic floor muscles compressed, breaking the speculum while it was still inside you. We checked for damage, but aside from some internal bruising, you should be fine to leave."

"Is Diana okay?" I ask.

"She had to go home. It seems she must have taken something, and it reacted badly."

Taken something? Ok, now I know they are hiding something.

"What do you mean by taken something? Did she say she saw something during the examination?"

Doctor Hendini's eyebrows raise and her reaction told me everything I needed to know.

"Why would you say that, Miss Roberts? Have you been seeing things?"

Shit. I better cut this short before more questions get asked.

"I just mean, did you find anything during the examination, Doctor?"

She gives me a sceptical look, then lets out a sign before answering me.

"Aside from the accident with the speculum, everything looks normal from what I could see. But I took samples to send for testing and will refer you to the pain clinic. I am worried about what happened. The amount of pain you were in for a simple examination is not normal. So, I will let your consultant know and we can go from there."

"How long before I hear?"

I watch her pause for a moment; her eyes are kind now as she rests her hand on mine.

"You know that a hysterectomy may not solve all these issues. Endometriosis is a hormonal issue too; this could stay with you even if we take away the reproductive organs. It's a big decision for someone your age, so please think carefully about what you are asking."

I have heard this speech before, so many times over the years. That or the male doctors telling me I should want to have a baby, that I'm still young. I was sick of hearing it. After three miscarriages and four failed relationships, this spiel is getting fucking old. I can already feel my blood boiling, as she again looks at me with that stupid, pitiful gaze.

"No offense, but I know my body, and I know what I want. You want me to suffer until I may or may not have a baby, fine? But I am done."

"That is not what I meant, Miss Roberts. Please calm down."

"No, I get it now. Operations are reserved for those who need them, as this is not life-threatening. I just have to wait in line like everyone else. But I thought as a woman doctor you would understand my pain. I was so stupid," I rant.

"No, Miss Roberts, that is not the case. We just want you to understand that surgery is a last resort."

I can hear the defiance in her tone, the same tone I have heard from every doctor over the years. The same condescending tone, that they know better because they are doctors, and I snap.

"DO YOU THINK THIS IS THE LIFE I WANT?! IF THIS WAS YOUR DAUGHTER SUFFERING AND BEGGING FOR HELP, WOULD YOU SEND HER AWAY AND TELL HER TO JUST SUCK IT UP!"

She doesn't answer. I throw the sheets aside and rip off the paper band. Her eyes are glued to the floor as I stumble out of the bed and grab my coat.

"Please, Miss Roberts, you have to understand that this is nothing personal. Please lower your tone or I will have you escorted out of the hospital."

"Oh, don't worry, I'm gone. We have nothing more to say to each other," I sneer.

I grab my stuff and race towards the exit to the ward. I can hear her calling after me, but I've stopped listening now. Nothing she can say will make a difference. As soon as I get downstairs and burst through the exit, I bawl my eyes out in front of the hospital. Tears and snot cascade down my face as I mourn the last hope I had.

I feel defeated as the frosty night air hits my skin. I can feel my tears freezing on my face. The snow has come early, blanketing the car park around me. I feel despair as I stare up at the blank sky. I just want to be heard. I just want this to be over. I want my life back.

"I am sorry, Cali," Meigs mutters. "But I tried to tell you if you want something done, you're better off doing it yourself."

Her tone seems more hushed, less harsh than usual, as she can sense the overwhelming turmoil I'm experiencing.

Does she? Care about me?

"Of course I do. You are my host. I just want to help you get stronger and, in the process, help me get stronger, too. If you listen and trust me, Cali. I promise I will leave, and you will never feel pain again."

Her voice is sincere. She means what she is saying. My options for going private disappeared the moment I went on sick leave. My last hope was that the doctors would help me and take me seriously. But that has been taken away from me too, so what other options are there? What hope do I have fighting against her alone? I'm desperate now. Evil or not, Meigs has kept her word. Everything she has said has always passed as truth. Maybe for once I should listen to my body and give it what it wants.

"I will ask you again Calico, do you trust me?"

"Yes," I whisper.

"Good, then let's take a walk, my friend. I know exactly what we need."

10:

We didn't walk far before hearing a scream coming from one of the side roads. Instead of giving in to my anxiety or running the other way, I pursue the sound of terror. Let my feet walk through the darkness down the cement path, blood rushing into my ears as my heart pounded against my rib cage.

What am I walking into?

The screams got louder as I rounded the corner. The streetlamp illuminates a couple at the corner of the street. A young woman was on the ground, being beaten up by another larger woman. The bigger lady was pushing the girl's head into the snow. She must have been a teenager. The sound of snow crunching under my feet was masked by the yelling and crying of the girl on the floor.

"Get up, you nasty little bitch!" the woman cries.

She kicks the girl in the stomach, over and over. I watch the violence unfold as blood from the young blonde mixes with the snow. Her hair is ragged and wet. The poor thing was squealing for the woman to stop. Instead, the plump beast lobs a beer can at her head.

"While you live under my roof, you'll do as you're fucking told!" She screams.

Before the woman can land another strike to her ribs, I find myself standing right behind her. A surge of power flows through my body like poison, and my hand grabs her chunky wrist. The woman turns and faces me.

Jesus, her monstrous actions match her form. She stinks of piss and alcohol.

"Who the fuck are you!?" she snarls.

"Just a passer-by," I simply answer.

"Well, fuck off and pass by. This has fuck all to do with you."

The girl is crying into the snow on her hands and knees, clutching her stomach and shaking. She looks up at me, a fresh string of blood drips from her bottom lip as she looks up at me.

"Are you deaf? I said piss off!" the woman roars in my face.

Her spittle smacks against my cheek, and an instant feeling of disgust overtakes me.

"Mom… please leave it. Stop."

Mom? This behemoth is doing this to her kid? Here's me, unable to hold a child to term and this twisted bitch is beating on hers in the street? What the hell is wrong with her?

"SHUT UP, YOU LITTLE WHORE! I'LL DEAL WITH YOU IN A MINUTE."

The skinny slip of a girl cowers in the snow, terrified. The woman turns her attention back to me, her eyes intense as she puffs out her chest and cracks her knuckles.

"You must be stupid then. I guess you want your face smashed in, too," she scoffs.

I feel intense pain, but it surges into my arms and legs. I feel like my ankles are gonna buckle from the pressure, but instead, my eyes glaze over. It's like I am now trapped inside my body, looking out through the eyes but not able to do anything. Just like before with the mugger in the park, I am just a Bia standard now. Before I lose complete control, I say something aloud from my lips.

"Run."

The woman bursts out laughing, the fleshy rolls of skin jiggling in time with laughter.

"I am not running nowhere, love, you must be fucking high!" she cackles.

"She wasn't talking to you."

That alien voice from before, Meigs. She has taken over my body again. This time, I actually want her to inflict as much pain and damage as possible on this sadistic cow.

"You heard her, girl," her voice directed at the teenager on the ground. "Run."

The girl's eyes shoot up to my body and she looks back at me with pure fear. Before finally scrambling up off the floor and making a run for it.

"COME BACK HERE, YOU LITTLE SLUT!" the woman roars.

She goes to turn away from me. I know she intends to pick a fight with the girl. To no doubt wail on her some more.

We cannot let that happen.

I hear a loud thwack noise and the woman flies into the wall by the pavement. Bricks tumble on top of her. I didn't even see my body move. Did that punch of energy come from me? From *her* using my body? Before I have a chance to form my next question. My body is moving toward the crumpled-up body next to the rubble. The large woman's top is torn, showing a badly drawn rose tattoo and there's a wet patch by her crotch that could be snow or piss. Honestly, I wasn't interested in finding out. Meigs seemed to be having a ball. I wasn't going to interfere.

The woman coughs blood into the snow. Blood pours from an open wound on her head where she hit the wall. I watch my hands grab both sides of her face, and her pupils dilate when I look down at her.

"Mother is god in the eyes of a child, you don't deserve that title," Meigs sneers.

I watch on as my hand's grip harder on both sides of her face. The woman sobs and begs through bleeding gums, and without warning, her face is bashed against what's left of the wall. Over and over until the skulls shatter into tiny pieces, bits of gore and cranium stick to the brickwork. The sound of bone crunching echoes in my ears. Brain matter pours out of what is left of her head. Like egg yolk, it drips onto the floor as her body falls to the snowy path.

I feel my senses return, clenching my blood-covered hands, to be sure. Looking down at the ground saturated in the woman's crushed skull and blood, not even the smell of snow can hide the musty smell emanating from her body. I can almost taste the metal in the air. I look at the puddle of pink stringy brain matter. Something is nestled away in the centre, calling to me. My mouth salivates when I notice a small lump that my eyes can't peel away from.

"You can see it now, can't you?" Meigs's voice is crystal clear in my mind.

"Why is it making me hungry?" I ask, drool dripping from my lip.

"That, Cali, is the hypothalamus connected to the pituitary gland. It controls hormone distribution. We need that. You eat that and I promise you, the pain will dissipate."

Her explanation made sense. The last thing I ate was also for hormone distribution. So, it makes sense that the main one I needed to stop my endo tissue from growing was to overload the hormone distribution part of my brain. Well, it didn't make sense, but looking at it made me want to dig in. Like this primal urge had been woken within me.

"Scoop it into your pockets. We have to go. I didn't intend to draw this much attention," Meigs commands.

I do as instructed. Without hesitation, I scoop the brain matter into my pockets and make a run back down the street opposite. Keeping the scene of gore and horrors as far away from us as possible. I never imagined that I would be a person to watch and do nothing. Most people will look at the situation and fall to pieces, but technically, this is the second murder I have been an accomplice to. Yet this time, I didn't even shed a tear. I feel numb, but not from the cold.

It's almost like my body and mind have separated themselves from the situation. Once I know there is a fair distance between me and the crime scene, I take a second to catch my breath. For the first time, I do not know how long I have run. Usually, two flights of stairs would kill me, but I just ran half a mile according to my Fitbit.

Fucking thing just congratulated me for beating my personal best.

I slip my hand into my pocket. It's still warm and feels like I've dipped my fingers into a tub of slim. I pull out a chunk of the brain and pop it into my mouth. The moment I start chewing, a flash of endorphins hit me. I feel amazing, like I could run a marathon or climb a tree, but right now I would just settle for getting home.

I must have walked over 8 miles, completely pain-free with no fatigue or back pain. It was like I was a teenager again, before this bullshit disease tore apart my body and left me the shell of a human being. I am still full of energy when I get into the lift; I pull the keys from my jeans and get ready to enter my flat. The doors open and I am greeted by a familiar face, my neighbour from across the hall.

Shit, of course, she walks the dog around this time every morning.

"Hey stranger," she chirps, "Haven't seen you in ages, you okay?"

I didn't even have time to answer before her German shepherd, Dash, who usually is very fond of me, growls at me, teeth bared, and his ears pinned back. I step out of the lift and the dog snaps at me.

"What the hell are you doing, you idiot! It's only Cali. Pack that in!"

But Dash is in full defence, acting as if I am a complete stranger. His fur stands on end as I pass him cautiously to get to the door. My neighbour has to practically drag him into the lift. As Dash barks furiously at me, I quickly get my keys and run into the flat. I think the entire building can hear Dash now. I slip down behind the closed door, wondering what the hell just happened.

Dash loves me, and always has, the entire time I've lived here. What the hell could have made him act so aggressively?

I reach into my pocket and remember the soggy brain still in my jacket pocket. The realisation hits me like a lorry, and I finally break down.

What the hell have I done?

11:

I stored the brain of the abusive woman in the fridge. No one comes to visit, so I did not have to worry about explaining it. Every time the pain reared its ugly head, I simply went to the fridge and had a snack on the hypothalamus. It actually helped with the pain, but some of the normal endo side effects remained the same. Such as the early morning diarrhoea run, but Meigs assured me that too would be gone with my next kill.

I tried not to think about it, emotionally I just created a wall between my reality and the things done between me and Meigs. Most people would have fallen apart or had a mental breakdown. But I had to look at things logically. I only killed two people.

One was in self-defence and the other was an abusive waste of human skin. I mean, who the hell beats up their own child? It still amazes me when I see stories about parents murdering their children. Yet there is me, a person who once loved the idea of having a baby, but now that dream is so far out of reach. I made peace with it a long time ago that it was never my fate to bear a child of my own.

For one, I never found the right man, but with this, how the hell are you supposed to have a relationship? Every single man I dated swore they could deal with it and would stand by my side. By the first year of being together, they were already throwing in the towel. I know many other women who have a similar condition to mine, who have loving, supportive partners and even had kids with them. The guy is there for every operation, and every doctor's appointment, never leaving their side.

But just like the situation with kids, I knew in my heart that until I had some form of normalcy with this, relationships would have to be another pipe dream. As an old-school romantic, I never thought I would ever give up on love. But that is what this disease does to you. It strips you of everything until there is nothing left but to accept that you will always be alone in your battle.

For me, at least, that is how it feels. I can't speak for others in my position. But I doubt they would go killing people for their hormone glands just to get some relief. But that's the thing, I don't really know whether anyone else has had the same experience. If they did, I doubt they would post about it on social media, because that would be a one-way ticket to a padded room in a psychiatric ward.

"You know that will only last you a couple more days, right?" Meigs comments.

Snapping me out of my internal monologue of thought. She has been pretty quiet for the last few days, so it is a surprise to hear her voice once more.

"How much more of this do I need to eat before it's enough?"

"Well," she muses, "Two kills so far, to get to full pain-free, I would say another six should do it."

"Six! Are you fucking serious? Why six?"

"Calm down Cali, we can pick easy targets if you let me take control," Meigs purrs.

"But you already have control? You take over my body when you kill people. How much more control do you want from me?" I snarl.

"You are dense, you know that? No wonder those guys got you into bed so easily," she hisses.

Ok, I will admit that insult did sting. Because I will admit at one point, I was stupid and believed anything I guy told or promised me.

But bringing it up as an insult was a low blow, even for her.

"When I take over, *YOU* are still there. This means your mind is not allowing me full access, but if you allow me to take over, it will be out of sight and out of mind."

"Why would I do that?"

I can hear her tutting inside my mind, along with a migraine brewing.

"Cali, I thought we passed this. You still do not fully trust me after all I've done for you?"

"Oh yeah, I really appreciate being a murderer."

A loud hiss resonated through my skull, and I felt something warm trickling down the inside of my leg. I look down and see a massive red patch forming on my jeans. Tapping the inside of my leg with my fingertips, I pull back when I notice the blood on them. Forcing me to waddle to the toilet, as expected, I pull my trousers down and see my jeans and underwear soaked with blood.

"No."

"That was just a warning Cali, don't make me bring on something worse or I will make sure your period is more than a month," Meigs growls.

I let out a heavy sigh, then I dump the bloody clothes in the hamper. The inside of my legs are slick with blood, so I need to wash it off. I turn the tap on and grab a flannel off the side, Meigs carries on chattering away in my brain as I wash.

"I need you to say yes, to agree to stay in your subconscious while I get what we need. Right now, you can only hear me because I can access your mind. But I cannot control your body without you watching it like a peeping Tom."

"So, what is it I have to do? Close off and let you have free rein? How do I know you don't want to take over completely and lock me away?"

I hear her sigh loudly as I dry off my legs. She takes a moment before answering me.

"I won't. I need you, remember? But if you insist on being a pain in my ass, then tonight you can watch again. But if you cannot hack it, then you need to step aside. Deal?"

It only takes a moment for me to consider this, but I nod to agree with her.

"Um, I am going to need verbal confirmation, remember? I don't have fucking eyes where I am."

"Shit, sorry. Yes, deal."

Maybe I should be more worried that I am making a deal to participate in watching a murder. But to be honest, from how I see it, it's nothing more than watching a movie.

I can only see the violence. I can't feel like the first time. I've watched worse horror movies and read harder-core horror than what she has done so far. Heck, I've read Simon McHardy and Sean Hawker. Now those guys are twisted. Whatever demented things she has planned, I'm pretty sure I've been desensitised to everything now.

"Ok, get dressed. I know where to head for the next meal."

12:

I decided on all black tonight and had to throw the other clothes down the shoot. Even with the bleach and stain remover, the blood would not come out. My coat is currently on a second cycle. Turns out brains are harder to get out of waterproof fabric than expected. So, I decided on something more conspicuous, also black. I look in the mirror and realise I look like a burglar. That or a rejection from a gangster music video, but considering the area. I am pretty sure no one will bat an eyelid.

"Enough daydreaming, Cali, time to leave," Meigs commands.

I throw on my shoes and head for the door, reluctant to open the door, especially after what happened with Dash. He seems to growl whenever he comes near my door now. I listen carefully as I unlock the door. No barking, so she must be out with him for a walk. I close the door behind me and decide to take the stairs. I cannot run into anyone tonight. When I reach the ground floor, I use the back way out of the tower block. Under the cover of darkness, I let Meigs guide me. My focus is sharp, scanning around the streets. I'm all alone. The streetlights illuminate my path towards the back streets. I have a feeling that we will be going further afield this time, probably so there is no way to connect the area. I can feel a fire burning inside of me, a mix of adrenaline and anxiety about the unknown.

I can see the lights are getting less. We seem to be heading for a woodland area. I can hear it. At first, I thought it was my heartbeat that I could hear in my ears.

The heartbeat is getting louder as we head towards an old church. The spire reaches up into the night sky and looks like it is just touching the full moon. The sound is loud, almost deafening now. I listen and let it lead me across to the cemetery right in the back. The moonlight casts shadows across the ground from the tombstones. It's an eerie sight, even for me I never felt more unsettled than I did passing a graveyard. I look ahead and there in the distance is a figure, kneeling over by one of the freshly dug graves. I'm quiet with every step I take, making sure not to disrupt the earth as I walk. The closer we get, the clearer her image becomes, a young girl kneeling before the small wooden cross, praying. Her long dark hair flows over her hood, as prays silently on the dirt pile.

There is something familiar about her. I can't place where I know her from, but that hair is familiar to me.

Where do I know this girl? Why is she so familiar to me?

I get this feeling inside my gut; I feel uneasy as I approach her. Something feels off, but I can't place why. I'm standing behind her now, looking down at her meek form. She hasn't noticed me yet. Meigs pushes me back into my subconscious. Allowing her control of my body, so I wait and watch as she stalks her prey using my body. I hear a gasp and realise she has noticed my shadow on the ground.

She turns and faces me; I realise how I know her the moment I see her eyes look into mine.

"Hello, Diana," Meigs announces.

The nurse from the hospital, but how? How did Meigs find her and why are we here? Did Meigs know all along?

The same fear I saw in her eyes that day reappears on her face. She makes the sign of the cross over her heart and mutters the lord's prayer under her breath. Inside my prison, I am screaming at Meigs, begging her not to do this. I feel like I'm pounding invisible fists against a wall, crying out that she be spared.

"Sorry Cali, but this one saw me," she replies.

She pulls the gold cross from Diana's neck and slices her throat with the point. The poor girl gargles blood as the slit gets wider, blood pours down her top, colouring it crimson. Gasping for air only makes it worse, as the blood pumps like a stream from the open gash. One hand already wrapped around her throat; she reaches out with the other. I want to grab her hand. Comfort her, stop the bleeding any way I can. I want to save her, but I know it is too late. I am responsible for her death.

I caused this.

"I knew you wouldn't have the stomach," Meigs gloats.

She pushes the girl onto her back. Diana's head drops onto the wood cross. It pierces the back of her skull, makes a sickening crunch as it breaks the base of her cranium. I look on in shock when I realise tonight's meal is not brains.

She yanks down the girl's trousers, tugging away her pants a little to reveal the V shape of her pelvis. Meigs leaves the opening of her vagina covered, allowing her one last shred of modesty. She takes the wooden stake from the grave next door and stabs it into her belly button.

I just heard her whimper, oh my god the poor girl is still alive!

I can hear her struggling to breathe. Her body shakes as the stake is pulled out and Meigs reaches inside the large chasm she has created. I want to close my eyes and look away, but they are pinned open. I have to watch this poor girl be disembowelled alive. Her face contorted in pain and terror, as my hands are being used to rummage inside her.

She doesn't deserve this; all she did was show me kindness. This shouldn't be her fate!

I can see something moving against the skin of her pubic area.

Horror-stricken when I realise that is where my hands have ended up, I can feel my face smiling. It looks like tentacles moving around under the skin, not fingers. I feel sick. I want to throw up in my mouth, but I have no power. I watch helplessly as her ovarian sack and fallopian tubes are yanked violently out of the hole and splatters onto her chest in a mangled, bloody mess.

Finally, I can breathe again; I look down at the dead body of Nurse Diana. The remains of her reproductive organs sit on top of her breasts. I stifle my sobs as I sit frozen in shock at the sight, staring at the woman whose only sin had been cared for me. I can hear her; that disgusting creature snickering inside me, pleased with her handy work. I watch the last of the blood dribble from Diana's throat.

"That was quite a workout," Meigs jokes.

"Why... why her?" I sob.

"I already told you; she saw me. She was marked for death the moment she laid eyes on me."

"She wouldn't have said anything. She was terrified. For fuck's sake, you could have let her live."

My sobbing became louder and harder to control. I let this happen. If she had never been in that exam room, she could have lived. I'm just as much a monster as Meigs.

"Will you quit your wailing? Someone will hear you," she snaps.

I look down at the ovaries resting on her chest, caked in blood and torn ligaments. I know if I waste them, she dies for nothing.

"Will you hurry and eat? I am starving."

13:

I step through the door with a sealed baggie of Diana. I'm disgusted with myself; I could disassociate myself from the horrors when the victim had no name.

I place her remains in the fridge and close the door. Not wanting to acknowledge that the life taken to ease my suffering was a good person. Everything goes in the washing machine; I stroll naked through the flat to the bathroom to wash away the sins of the night. The hot water scolded my skin as I curl up in the bath and sob uncontrollably.

"I told you, you were not ready for this," Meigs spits.

"What does it matter?" I reply, "Now I am a monster, just like you."

I hear her scoff.

"Monster? You don't know the meaning of the word."

I rest my head on my knees, looking over at the toilet. The one place most of my life has been spent, never dreamed of devouring people's insides just to get past it. My bladder seems to have returned to what it used to be, not getting the frequent urge to piss or pass watery shit.

I look down between my legs. A mound of hair has grown. The lumps around my labia have dissipated, and no scar left behind, which is unusual. But what part of this situation is not unusual? I look down at the scars and back towards the opening. My focus is now on something moving from between my legs. I lean over to take a better look.

Fear swells through me when I see a large wiggling appendage moving in the water. A tentacle sloshing about in the water. I let out a yelp and crawl backward. The single wiggling arm still moving had detached itself from inside me. I lean forward to poke it with my index finger; it feels squishy and looks a reddish brown. It reminds me of the clots I pass when I'm on my period, but it's long with tiny suckers attached to it, reminding me of an octopus limb. It's not a hallucination, it's very real.

"Oh, don't mind that." Meigs comments, unphased. "The change is taking place, so I'm losing some pieces I don't need."

"Wait, this is part of you?!"

"I guess you call them adhesions, nodules. But essentially, these are the bits that hurt you. So, it looks like things are coming along nicely."

"You said I am not your first? What did you mean by that?"

She falls silent for a moment, giving me a chance to scuttle out of the bath. Away from the thing dissolving in the bath water and swirling down the drain. I scrub my skin until it's red with the towel, washing my finger twice after the interactions.

"I've been here before, with different bodies at different times. But no one has ever heard my voice before. You are the first to hear me, the first one who listened."

Well, that's not the least bit comforting. If I wasn't able to hear her, then I wouldn't be in this fucking mess.

"Three more, and I promise you will never have to worry about pain ever again," Meigs promises.

What choice do I have? I have already come this far. I might as well see it through to the end now. I go back to my room; I'm determined to get in my pyjamas. I notice my phone is lit up with a voicemail. It's the hospital.

No doubt to tell me again about the long waiting list or to advise on more drugs to shove down my throat.

I'm too exhausted to deal with their bullshit. I crawl across the bed and push the pyjamas aside. I roll up into the comfy duvet until it completely envelopes me like a burrito. I just want to shut the world out.

"You get some rest, Cali. I promise to not disturb you."

"And the deal?" I ask, exhausted.

"It stands. Leave everything to me now. You just keep eating what I bring. You never have to worry about killing."

My eyes feel heavy as I drift into a deep sleep. I hear a distant sound of laughter fading into nothing.

"Just leave it all to me."

14:

I'm trapped in my nightmares. I want to wake up, but my eyes won't open. Visions of unimaginable horrors swamp my brain. The first image is a young girl with dirty blonde hair walking down a dark back street. The cold air makes her breath come out in a mist, which is no surprise considering what she is wearing. A short mini skirt, fishnet stockings held up by a garter belt and a thin tank top.

It doesn't take a genius to realise she is a prostitute in the worst area of London. She barely looks fourteen, her high heels clicking against the pavement as she passes row after row of convenience stores. I hear a wolf whistle and see a group of drunk men pursue her. My heartbeat rages in my ears as she runs, and the men chase her down the backstreet. My anxiety is at its peak as one man catches up to her, grabbing her by the wrist.

She turns and his fist connects with her jaw, forcing her to the ground, sobbing. The other two men watch the entrance to the side pavement while the bigger tattooed man sits on top of her. She tries screaming for help, but he has her pinned to the floor. His hand across her mouth while the other fumbles with the zip on her dress. Tears pour down her face with blood from the fresh cut on her cheek.

I can't watch, I want to look away. But my eyes are pinned to the scene as he tugs her skirt down and unbuckles his belt. Someone has to stop this, someone has to step in.

For fucksake, can no one hear her screaming?

He pulls down his pants, and his hard member bounces free, ready to do the unspeakable.

Then the screaming stops and her eyes are looking behind his shoulder. Horror and fear all in one look.

Is she? Is she looking at me?

Before I can react, his shaft goes flying from his hand. Blood splatters all over his exposed balls and he cries out in agony. His body is flung away from her, landing against the wall like a rag doll. He is limp, aside from a couple of twitches, and barely makes any other movements. His eyes are pissing blood, and I watch as whoever has intervened casually strolls toward him.

His blue eyes are blank, frozen in a state of terror. The hand of the defender reaches down and yanks his balls from the mess of bloody public hair. I hear a crunch, like someone biting into an apple. To my utter disgust, the testicle comes into view again, a massive chunk torn out of it. A white substance leaks from the exposed sack and mixes with the blood.

I want to throw up. This is rancid. The girl! Where is she?

As if hearing my thoughts, the vision moves to the girl curled up on the ground, still sobbing. Her body is frozen in terror as she looks at the corpse of her would-be attacker. She shuffles back on her bum across the alley, trying to put as much distance as she can between her and them. Her ankle is twisted with the bone sticking out. She isn't running anywhere.

The sound of her terrified heartbeat thumps in my head as she cries and begs the saviour to be spared. I can't hear what she is saying. The pounding in my head is too loud to make out any of her words. She doesn't look grateful; she looks like a deer being stalked by another lion. Trembling on the ground in a pool of her piss.

No, don't please stop. Don't hurt her.

My pleas are left unheard, as the poor girl is sliced open. Her guts pour onto the asphalt and a hand reaches inside her, yanking out her intestines until they are a splayed mess across the ground. Blood pouring from her mouth, the hand reaches in again and digs around inside her. I feel like I am watching Jack the Ripper, as her stomach and liver are flung to the side, and the hand finally snags a pink fleshy V-shaped organ out of her.

It wriggles between her killer's fingers like jelly. The closer I look, the more familiar the organ becomes.

That's... her... no, it can't be. It looks like her uterus...

I wake up finally and scream the place down.

15:

I can hear banging on the front door. I jump into trousers and a top and rush over. Unlocking the door, I pull it open to see Maria at the door.

"Are you ok? I heard you screaming. Do I need to call an ambulance?" she asks, panicked.

Screaming? Oh god yeah, she must have heard me.

"No, no, I am fine, Maria. Just had a bad dream, and it freaked me out. I am so sorry If I woke you up."

She gives me a confused look.

"Well, no, it's four in the afternoon, Cali. I was just coming in from work."

"Oh."

Wait? Four in the afternoon. How long have I been asleep?

"Are you sure you're, ok? I mean, we haven't seen you in weeks. We are all pretty worried."

Maria has a look of genuine concern across her face.

"Yeah, I've been dealing with a lot lately."

"Have the doctors got back to you? Hopefully, with good news?"

Her eyes rest on my waist, getting wider the longer she stares.

I wish it was that easy, love. Everyone always assumes it's an easy fix.

"Listen, I'm not feeling great. I'm gonna have to lie down."

"Oh, of course. Let me know if you need anything," Maria says with a smile.

She is still standing there as I close the door, her eyes full of sadness.

I breathe a sigh of relief.

I don't have the energy to have a full conversation with you anymore. Especially after the nightmare, along with how disorientated I feel.

"Wait, what day is it?" I wonder out loud.

I run back into the bedroom and reach over to the table for my phone. I can't believe what I'm seeing on the screen. It says it's the twenty-ninth.

I've been asleep for two weeks. No, that can't be right!

I can see numerous missed calls and messages from work and the surgery. I've missed so much; I think back to the dreams I've been having, wondering if they were really dreams now.

Two weeks without food or toilet breaks seem so unlikely. My trousers feel tight around my stomach, although with the bloating I get, that wasn't unusual.

I look down and have to hold back the shock. Now I know why Maria looked at me with such concern.

My stomach is the size of a beach ball. I must look about nine months pregnant. Which is clearly impossible, as I haven't been sexually active in years because of my diagnosis. I pull up my top to see an enormous mass has formed under my skin. I can't even see my pelvis anymore, or my feet, for that matter.

I'm stuck to the spot, glaring down at this bump attached to me. When it moves, I feel my body shake.

What the fuck is this?

"You're awake!" Meigs cheers. "I thought you would never regain consciousness."

"What the fuck is this?" I wail.

"The final stage Cali, soon all your pain will be a thing of the past. You have one last thing to do."

"What?"

"Go into the kitchen and eat the last of the glands. Once you have eaten, we can begin."

I do as commanded and head into the kitchen. I open the fridge and suck in a large amount of air. Every part of my body is stiff, my hand clamped on the door as I see three empty containers covered in blood.

The fourth container had some leftover gore stuck to the side of the plastic; it looks like what I saw in my dream.

"Eat what's left of the left fallopian tube for me, Cali," she coos.

I reach in and grab the container, pulling the lid off and placing the contents in a bowl on the side. I look at the purple-coloured string of the organ; the staring contest between me and it seems to last ages. I finally suck it down like spaghetti, it makes a disgusting slurping noise as it passes my lips.

I lean over the counter, and my stomach stretches, looking bigger than before.

"Now what?"

Silence. Meigs doesn't answer.

"Meigs, now what?"

Again, I am met with an eerie silence, then unimaginable pain shoots through my belly. Water pours down my legs like someone has turned the tap on. Contractions of unbearable pain come and go in the space of minutes, forcing me onto my knees by the oven. I try to hold back from crying out in pain. I can't let the neighbours get involved in this.

Whatever this is.

Another wave of pressure in my vagina, then another. My stomach moves constantly as the contractions make me bleed out through my trousers.

"Take off your trousers, Cali. It has begun."

**

I lay on my back against the cold floor with my lower half completely exposed. As I embrace the blinding pain between my legs, I can feel my cervix stretching and my organs shifting around.

I look at my reflection in the filthy oven glass. I look gaunt and pale as a ghost. Almost skeletal in appearance. But my face is still round. Over the years, this condition has worn me down to the shell of the person I was. The realisation brings me to tears and I cry out when the next contraction tears through my abdomen.

"You said there would be no more pain!" I wail.

"Just hold on Cali. This is the last step. You need to push when I tell you," Meigs urges.

Please, I want this to be over with, make the pain stop. I feel like I'm being ripped inside out.

"MAKE IT STOP!" I scream.

Blood gushes out of the gaping hole that used to be the opening to my vagina. It feels like someone is yanking open my inside. I won't make it.

"PUSH NOW," Meigs commands.

My brain is on fire as her yelling echoes around my cranium. Telling me to keep pushing through the agony, I can hear my flesh tearing beneath me.

Blood surrounds me on the floor as I keep pushing with all the force my muscles can stand. I'm lightheaded and my eyesight is going fuzzy. I can't see straight anymore as everything blurs.

"One more push," she whispers to me.

I grab the spoon off the floor and bite down so as not to scream out like a banshee. The force I use cause my teeth to crack with the pressure.

One more push and everything goes black.

"Well done," I hear her say.

My eyes open and they feel sticky and heavy, and my fingers and joints feel smaller. When things finally come into focus, I see my face looking down at me. I cry and it sounds like the cry of a newborn baby. I lift my hand and it is the size and shape of a baby.

How? How did I become this?

"Hush, Cali, it's alright no more crying now."

That voice is my voice, that face with a kind smile looking down over me. It's me, that is my body, so why am I outside of it?

"I imagine you have so many questions," she says while rocking my tiny, fragile body.

Too many, why am I like this? Why are you inside my body? How did you take over my skin?!

"I am sorry, sweetheart, but I cannot hear you anymore. I imagine, though this is both terrifying and confusing, you gave me consent. You let me take over. You allowed your illness, me, define you. The moment that happened, you lost everything."

She's walking with me in her arms. I gargle some noises to try to speak. A stiff wind blows past my naked body, and I shiver in her grip. With one hand, she pushes the window open while still holding me in the other.

Both hands now back around my tiny form, she reaches out with me in them. I look to the side. Oh my god, I'm out the window.

WHAT THE FUCK IS SHE DOING!

I'M JUST A BABY, WHY IS SHE HOLDING ME OVER A SEVEN-STORY DROP? Don't YOU DARE MEIGS, DON'T, PLEASE!

I WANT TO LIVE! I WANT TO LIVE!

"Shhh, Cali, it is all going to be ok. I promised you no more pain." Her face is contorted with a sinister smile as she speaks.

"One moment of pain now, for an eternity of peace," she sneers.

I let out a terrified cry from the very depths of my newly formed lungs, bawling my eyes out.

Please, it can't end like this.

All I wanted was to be free of the pain and live a normal life. Find love, have children, be like everyone else. This is the price you pay for disregarding everything, for giving up, and letting the darkness in. I know that now, it's just too little, too late.

She releases me from her grasp, and I can feel my body falling through the air, my tiny legs and arms flailing about as the ground gets closer and closer...

Dedications

To all my those fighting their own demons who get up every day, battling the monster within. Whether mental or physical, you can win. Never Give up, you are stronger than you realise.

Thank you to Ash Ericmore for the amazing cover, as well as his heartfelt support. Candace, thank you for your time and the love you have shown this very personal to me.

ABOUT THE AUTHOR

Nat Whiston

Nat Whiston is from Birmingham, England, and started her writing journey with submissions in Black Ink anthologies. Published her first short story What's Eating You on Godless Horrors and did a collaboration story with Ash Ericmore - Your Move. Has the first novel of her three-part Extreme Horror/Dark Fantasy series out called, Death Walks with Me. Published a Bizzaro horror called The Wilderness and has her own kid's series with Little Cape Publishing, called Niko's Nightmare Portal Pet. She also does Nat Whiston Reviews, to support other authors in the indie community, with co-host Creepy Bunny. Her favorite author is Clive Barker.

Printed in Great Britain
by Amazon